Walking
to School

by Eve Bunting
Illustrated by Michael Dooling

Clarion Books
a Houghton Mifflin Company imprint
215 Park Avenue South, New York, NY 10003
Text copyright © 2008 by Eve Bunting
Illustrations copyright © 2008 by Michael Dooling

The illustrations were executed in oil on canvas.
The text was set in 16-point Carré Noir Demi.

www.clarionbooks.com

Printed in Malaysia

Library of Congress Cataloging-in-Publication Data

Bunting, Eve, 1928–
Walking to school / by Eve Bunting ; illustrated by Michael Dooling.
p. cm.
Summary: When the path to eight-year-old Allison's Catholic school goes through hostile
Protestant territory in Belfast, Northern Ireland, Allison finds she is not alone in her loathing of the situation.
ISBN 0-618-26144-3
[1. Belfast (Northern Ireland)—Fiction. 2. Northern Ireland—Fiction. 3. Prejudices—Fiction.] I. Dooling, Michael, ill. II. Title.
PZ7.B91527Wak 2007
[E]—dc22   2004022942

ISBN-13: 978-0-618-26144-4
ISBN-10: 0-618-26144-3

TWP   10 9 8 7 6 5 4 3 2 1

To those who, together, brought peace to Ireland
—E. B.

For Jane, as always
—M. D.

To those who, together, brought peace to Ireland
—E. B.

As soon as I wake up, I see the yellow wallpaper that Mum and I put up last week. My bedroom looks so nice. For a minute I'm happy, but then I remember yesterday, and I lie there, thinking about what happened. I start wondering about Protestants and Catholics. Do they hate each other as much in other countries as they do here in Northern Ireland? Mostly, I don't think about this kind of stuff, but how can I help it, after yesterday?

My mum is calling to me from downstairs. "Allison, love. Time to get up."

I squinch down under the blankets.

It's the second day of school, and I don't want to go. I wish I could stay safe in bed, but I can't. I wish I hadn't started this new school that my mum went to when she was my age. I wish we'd moved someplace else. But maybe the Protestants won't be there today, lying in wait for us.

I make myself get up.

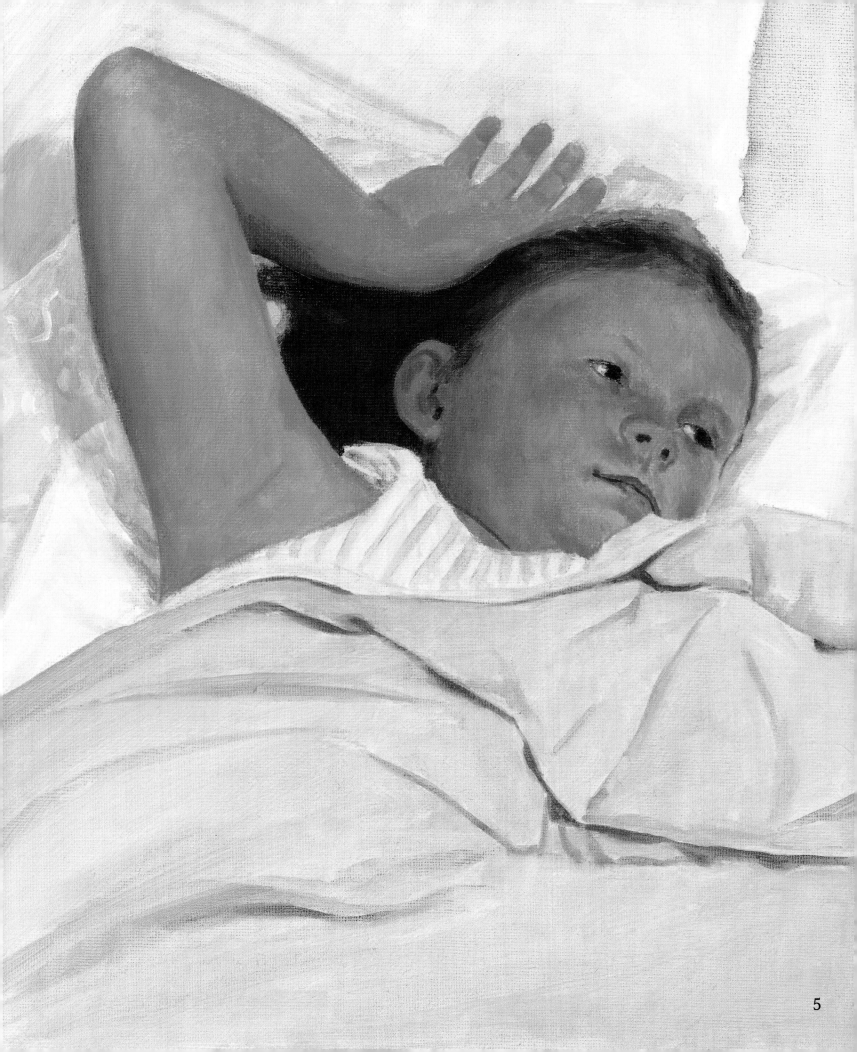

My school uniform is ready on the chair. I put it on. All summer I loved the thought of my new uniform, especially the blazer with the St. Claire's Primary School for Girls crest on the pocket and on the brass buttons.

I don't love it anymore.

On the dresser is my blue box. I take out my lucky tiger's-eye marble. I won it last year from John Sweeney, and I've won every game I've played with it since. When I hold it to the light, it gleams like darkest gold, streaked through with moving gray clouds. My tiger's-eye marble is my most favorite thing. I slip it in my blazer pocket and go slow as I can downstairs.

Mum says, "Good morning, lovey, and don't you look a picture!" She fills a bowl with cereal for me and ties one of her aprons around my neck so I won't spill on my new clothes.

"Is Daddy walking us to school?" I ask.

"No, pet. He couldn't take another day off. But your Uncle Frank's coming by."

I keep my head bent over my cereal. I love my Uncle Frank. I used to, anyway. I'm not sure if I do anymore. He's good to me. But I know something about him now that frightens me, something my mum and dad don't know.

One night I heard my Uncle Frank and his friends whispering in our kitchen when my parents were out and he was minding me. He thought I was asleep upstairs.

"Liam Connors has got to be taught a lesson," he'd said. And more awful things. His voice was cold and scary. I'd stood behind the living-room door, shivering in my nightdress.

I hear his key in the front door now, and my mum smiles. "Here's himself!" she says.

Uncle Frank comes into the kitchen, rubbing his hands together. "Cold as a frog's belly out there," he says.

"How are you doing?" he asks Mum, and then he turns to me: "How's my best girl?" He puts a bag of sugar almonds down in front of me.

"Och, Frankie, you spoil her," Mum says.

She pours him a cup of tea, and he drinks it standing up.

"Are we ready for the battle?" he asks, and I can tell he's looking forward to what may happen.

Uncle Frank is big and heavy. He has the bluest, laughingest eyes. Why did I have to hear what I heard that night?

"Did you see the pictures on the telly?" he asks Mum.

Mum nods. I keep on eating.

"It was great altogether," Uncle Frank says. "All those wee Catholic children trying to walk to their school, and all them big Protestant thugs throwing rocks at them and shouting insults. That'll show people what Protestants are really like."

I'd seen those Protestants yesterday morning myself, in person. Some of them had spat at us. I was lucky. None of the spit landed on me. But a big gob of it hit Annie McGowan's shoulder and sat there, all frothy and bubbly, till her mum wiped it off.

I don't want the rest of my cornflakes.

Uncle Frank sets down his cup. "Aye. They're a bad lot."

But are we a bad lot, too? I wonder. What about the things I heard Uncle Frank say that night? "Liam Connors has got to be taught a lesson. Going to a pub and talkin' to them Protestants."

"Maybe he's tellin' them too much about our business." That was John Bradley.

"I hear he's walking out with a Protestant girl." That was Henry McAfee.

There was a silence then while I listened to my heart thump.

"Tomorrow night," my Uncle Frank had said.

And a couple of the others had repeated, "Tomorrow."

I'd gone back up to bed, wondering what I'd heard and what it meant. Poor Liam, whoever he was. He was going to get in trouble.

Two days later a young fellow called Liam Connors was found, beaten senseless, in an alley off the Crumlin Road. He had both legs broken. My mum knew him a bit. He worked in a shop where she bought bread.

"It's terrible," she'd said. "And him such a nice wee lad."

I know my Uncle Frank had something to do with Liam Connors's getting beaten, and I can't stop thinking about it every time I see him.

"Are we ready?" he asks now, and my mum lifts the apron off me and smoothes my hair.

"We are," she says.

Uncle Frank drains his cup. "Let's go!"

Mum takes my hand when we go out on our street, and Uncle Frank marches in front of us, like a guard on duty. No need for a guard yet. There's no danger here where we live. It's all Catholic.

There are other kids heading for St. Claire's with their mums and dads, and we wait for each other so we can walk together down Drummond Street. There's a good crowd of us.

Drummond is Protestant territory, but we have to go along it to get to our school. That's the trouble. My mum says children going to St. Claire's always had to go this way. She and her friends walked along this street, but nobody bothered them then. It's as if Protestants and Catholics hate each other more now.

The Protestants who live on Drummond are lined up waiting for us. I can see them up ahead. I close my fist on my lucky marble in my pocket.

The noise is awful. They're blowing horns and whistles and clanging the metal lids of rubbish bins. Some of them are wearing scary Halloween masks. They're shouting stuff I don't want to hear. I want to put my hands over my ears, but I'd have to let go of my lucky marble.

"Eyes straight ahead!" my mum shouts at me. "Pretend they're not there."

But they are there.

There are lots more of them today than yesterday. Today there are kids, too.

The crowd's screaming stuff. There are plenty of bad cuss words flying. I'm eight years old and I've heard some of those words before, but what about the little kids? Some of them are just four. The Protestants have sticks, too, but they're only waving them. So far.

There are reporters walking backward in front of us. One is shouting into a microphone, "Tomorrow there will be soldiers here on Drummond Street to protect these little children on their way to school!"

"That's the stuff!" Uncle Frank screams. He's excited and happy. I'm pushing my way along. Suddenly, somebody grabs my blazer and tears off one of my buttons. I crouch down, trying to get it, but it's rolling away.

And then I see this girl, this Protestant girl about my age. She has on
pink high-top tennis shoes and she's down on her hands and knees,
crawling in among the Protestant feet. She wants my button! She wants
a Catholic souvenir. People are shoving at her. Somebody steps on

her hand. But she finds my button, picks it up, and then crawls toward me. She stands and holds it out to me. She has frizzy brown hair and she's wearing a navy blue sweater.

"Is this yours?" she asks.

"'Tis," I say. "Thanks."

I'd thought all wrong about her. And that makes me feel bad.

"Allison. Don't you be talking to her!" Mum still has my hand and she's tugging it.

Uncle Frank is ferocious. "Get away from her, you dirty Protestant!" he yells.

The girl takes a step back

"My mum made me come," she shouts to me. "I didn't want to. I hate this."

"Me, too." I take out the tiger's-eye marble from my pocket and call, "Here. This is for you. It's lucky." I have to stretch back to reach her hand.

Her fingers close around the tiger's-eye, and then she opens them and looks down at the marble. "Thanks," she says.

For a second or two I see the shine of it, the jungle colors, and I want to snatch it back. But I don't. I see the girl's fist close on it tightly, and then Uncle Frank jerks me away.

I look over my shoulder, though, and I can still see her. She's looking down at the marble, and then she lifts her head. She smiles at me and gives a small secret wave.

I give a small wave back.

Uncle Frank's mouth is set in a tight line. "Are you mad altogether, girl?" he says. "Getting friendly with the enemy!"

"Who says she's the enemy?" I mutter.

29

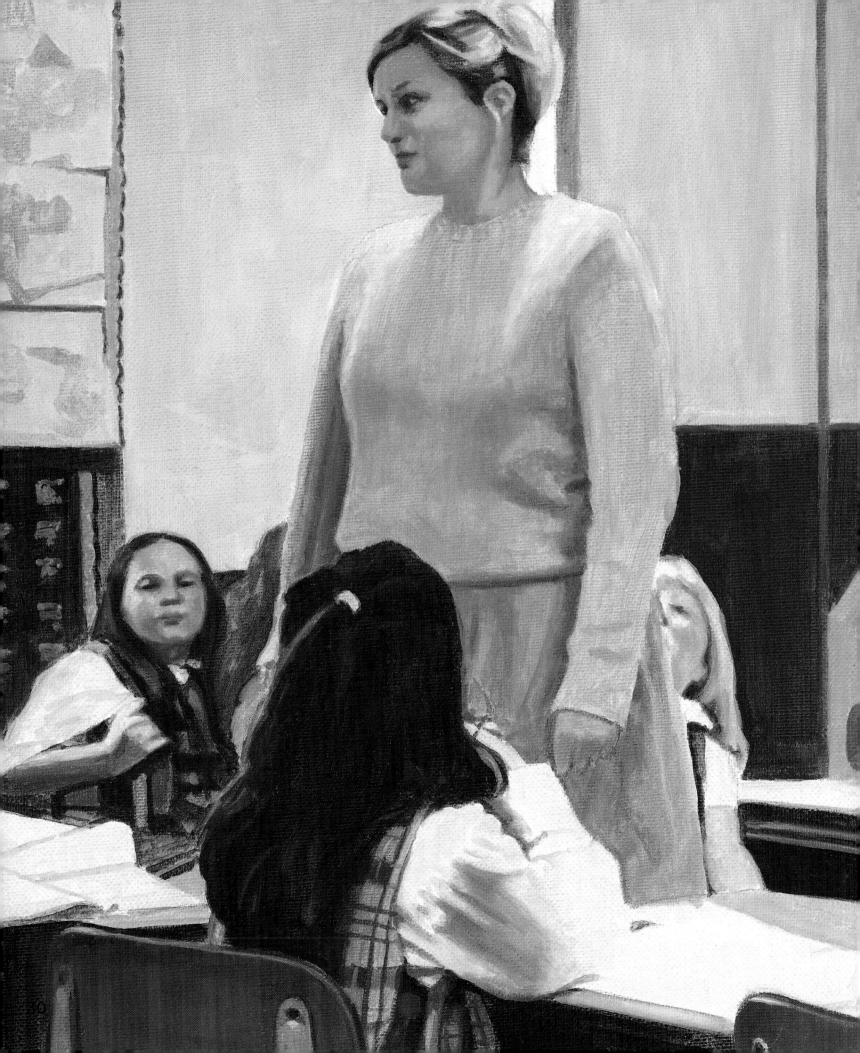

We get to school and I sit at my desk and Miss Gallagher asks if we're all right.

"We are, Miss Gallagher," we say and she nods, all serious, and says, "You're all Irish heroes, so you are."

I stare out of the window. What is she talking about? I don't feel like a hero. All I know is, I met a Protestant girl who was nice. She said she hated this fighting, and so do I. I think we could be friends, if we had the chance. I know we could.

If the grownups would let us.

Author's Note

This book was inspired by a sad happening in Belfast, Northern Ireland's major city, several years ago. A group of hostile Protestants harassed Catholic children on their way to school. The children were going through "Protestant territory."

The conflict between Catholics and Protestants in Northern Ireland is centuries old. The majority of people want to live in peace. But extremists on both sides kept "the Troubles" alive. Allison could as easily have been a Protestant child, walking to school through a Catholic neighborhood.

After many, many years of these "Troubles," a peace accord was agreed to in June of 2007. One hopes it will last and that events such as those in this book will be a thing of the past.